My Beach Adventure

My Beach Adventure: *A Cozy Spot Story*

PROMINENT
BOOKS
EDGE

5830 E 2nd St, Ste 7000 #9983
Casper, WY 82609
USA

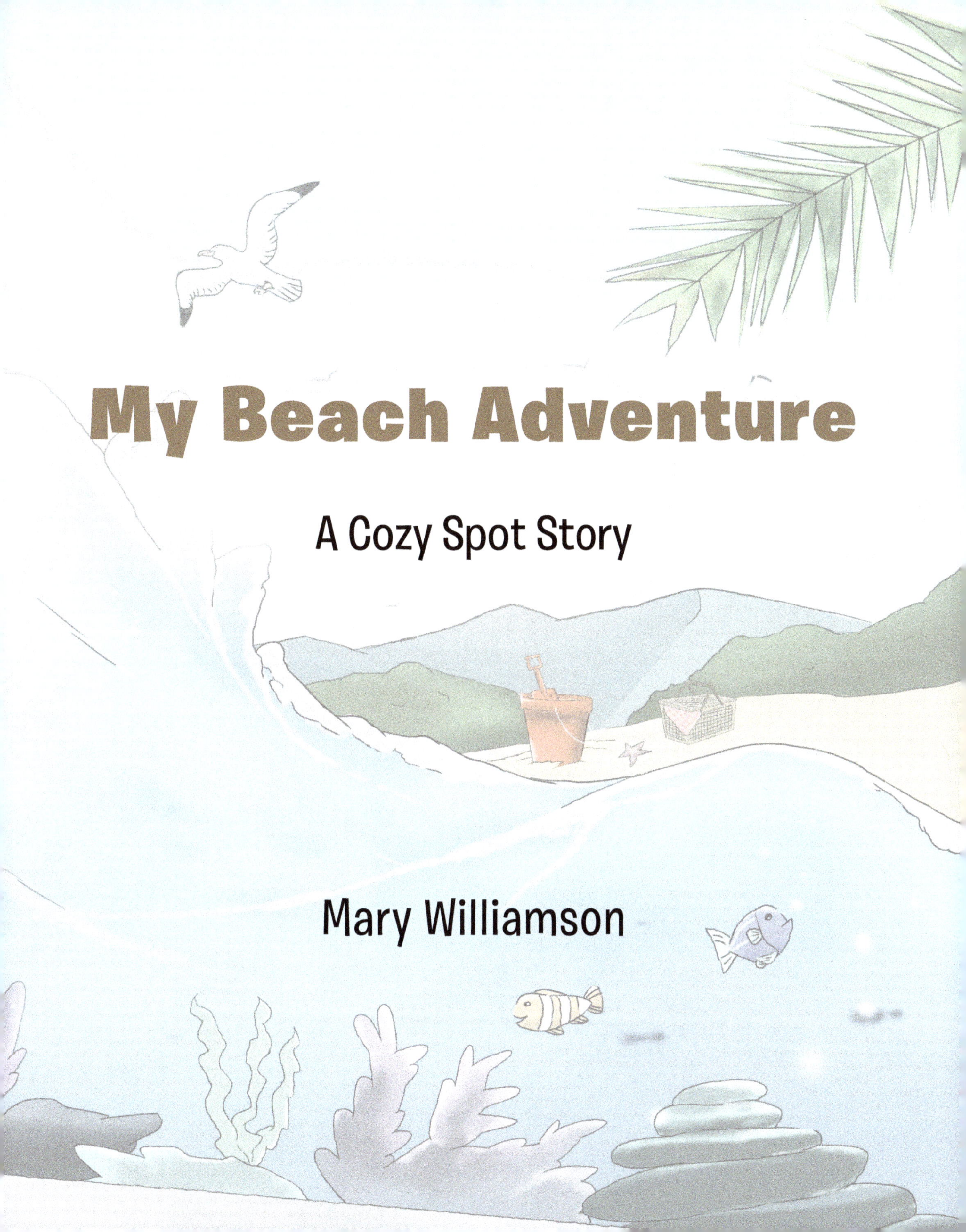

My Beach Adventure

A Cozy Spot Story

Mary Williamson

Tomorrow I am going to the beach! I wish I could go every day, but I only go at special times.

It will be a perfect day filled with sunshine. I know the beach will be beautiful!

I will bring my pail.

We'll pack up the car with a picnic basket and a colorful blanket. I like our red-and-white beach umbrella. It looks so snappy blowing in the breeze.

Daddy will set it up in the dry sand. It is good to have a little *shade* to sit in . . . between my searches for beach treasure!

Have you ever watched the sunshine making the water shimmer and dance?

Sun Block

The water looks so cool, but the sun on your face makes you feel warm. I do make sure to have sunblock on so that I don't get a sunburn. I try not to wiggle and giggle when my mom rubs the lotion on! Sometimes that's **_hard_**!

After we are settled in our cozy beach spot, I won't be able to _wait_ to start my treasure-hunting adventure. I love the feel of _wet sand_ under my feet when I walk along the edge of the water. I wonder what's **under** the sand. Maybe I'll **DIG** there. I have a little shovel.

I would never go **INTO** the water without a grown-up! But . . . I CAN splash. Maybe I'll dig up some shells! Who knows what is there waiting to be discovered?

Shells are houses for sea creatures. After they don't need them anymore, the shells sometimes wash up onto the beach, where you can find them! They are so beautiful.

There are lots of kinds of shells. I like to find different shapes, colors and sizes. What you can find depends on where the beach is. There are lake beaches and ocean beaches. All have different shells to find.

Sometimes you'll even find shells at the edge of a **river**. You will find so many when you start to look!

I will be at an *ocean* beach tomorrow. There are so many different things to discover . . .

Starfish, sand dollars and periwinkles are just a few.

I love periwinkles! They are teeny and often have a little hole in the shell. You can string them on elastic thread and give bracelets to your friends. The shells look like this . . .

Every time the waves come up onto the sand, there is a chance that shells will tumble onto my toes. I like that! I'll pick them up and put them into my pail.

Treasure!

I'd like to know about the creatures that used to live inside of the shells that I find. Maybe a grown-up shell lover will help me learn!

Some beach places don't seem to have a lot of shells . . . but there are ALWAYS smooth stones to find. Some are very colorful. I like the pink ones. Some look shiny and <u>very</u> special. Lots of people have stone collections, and I think I'll start one . . . .

People who really love collecting things that are hidden in the sand are called beachcombers! Isn't that a funny name?

I'm not really a **<u>serious</u>** beachcomber . . . but I really do like finding stuff in the sand!

When the waves crash on the beach, I'll see sea foam and will smell the wonderful salty air. There will be bubbles in the wet sand.

SEA SHELLS
LIVING BEACHES

Seagulls will walk back and forth, looking for little fish, and sometimes they will even find little *crabs* to eat. I guess seagulls are beachcombers too! When a **big** wave comes, they will scurry back to a safe place! They are such fun to watch!

Have you ever heard of beach glass? It is very hard to find, but when you do . . . it is very special. Beach glass is a **happy** thing that comes from **mistakes**. Sometimes broken bottles and glass things fall into the water, which is **NOT** a good thing!

I would **NEVER** litter, and I know you wouldn't either. But then . . . the waves and the underwater rocks take away the sharp edges.

Sometimes the smooth pieces wash up on the shore.

They look like jewels, and there are many colors to find. And, even if you don't find any, it is such fun to look for them!

We are going to have a picnic. Sometimes I don't want to stop what I am doing, but it is nice to have lunch with my friends and family and to show them what I have found!

My mom tells me that we will be having my favorite . . . peanut butter and jelly sandwiches. I will have to be careful that I don't get sand stuck in the jelly. Yuck!

After lunch I'll play in the sand. I can use my shells to decorate the sandcastles that my brother and I build!

I will make sure that I put those shells back in my pail before we leave the beach and before the waves wash them away.

I don't know what I'll find on our adventure tomorrow, but when I get home, I am going to find a little *box* for my found treasures. Every time I go to the beach. I will add more beautiful stones and pieces of beach glass and shells that I *collect*.

Maybe I will decorate the box. It has to be sturdy because I am thinking about gluing shells onto the top.

My treasure box will be a cozy spot for the special little beach treasures. They make me happy. So if one day the weather is gloomy, I can open my box and remember a **sunny** day with my family!

I am going to close my eyes now in my nighttime cozy spot and think about what fun we'll have tomorrow. I will go to sleep right away!

Good night! Sweet dreams!

A Note from the Author

The Cozy Spot books are bedtime stories for our little ones. They are a **celebration of simple all-American family activities** that are increasingly lost in our high-tech world. The tales are happy and magical and are meant to foster creativity as well as an awareness of nature.

They are written with love in ***The Cozy Spot Cottage*** Bluff-ton, South Carolina.